T0246956

GUNSLINGER

LONNY MEAD

Published 2023

Copyright 2023, Lonny Mead

All rights reserved. No part of this book may be reproduced or transmitted in any form or by any means, electronic or mechanical, including photocopying, recording, or by any information storage and retrieval system without the written permission of the author, except were permitted by law.

ISBN: 979-8-35093-889-0 paperback

ISBN: 979-8-35093-890-6 ebook

*This story is written for and dedicated
to my mother.*

Katheryn D. Peluso

"The biggest western movie fan in the world!"

ACKNOWLEDGEMENTS

I am very grateful and proud of my family for their support and love. Thank you Lewna Mulana, Nashia Mead, and Tristan Mead for all the beautiful artwork and encouraging ideas and amazing rap lyrics and studio performance on the Gunslinger songs.

A special thanks to Kay Lynn Golyer and Lindsey Cotton for their editing contributions to the book.

Special thanks to Jessica McKenzie for her vocal coaching and proofreading for the book.

Special thanks to Catheryn Rose Smith for her vocal coaching.

Gunslinger Misic Story

The Fictional Gunslinger book is the back story for the music story album titled "Gunslinger", both written and performed over a three-year period by artist known as Lonny Mead.

Special thanks to Lindon J Hugh's for his friendship, brilliant mixing and mastering skills, and amazing vocal harmonies.

Thank you, Will Braun, for your recording and engineering skills, the 808s and Keyboards.

My deepest gratitude to Walter Cross for
his spectacular drums and vision.

My heartfelt thank you to Stormy
Cooper and Stormy Cooper media.

I would also like to thank Jeffery Sweaengin
and Swearngin Guitars fort their hard
work on the Gunslinger guitar.

DISCLAIMER

The Gunslinger Story Album and book
took over 3 years to create.

Although the story is fiction, a tremendous amount
of time was invested in researching interesting
true events, places, and facts, that helped shape the
story while trying to maintain a geological and
chronological backdrop for the story. Even though
the Gunslinger story depicts a challenging time in
our history, it is merely just a good old fashioned
western story that was written with respect
given to all people, all race, and all cultures. The
Gunslinger is an epic adventure for all to enjoy.

GUNSLINGER

LONNY MEAD

CONTENTS

CHAPTER ONE

Gunslinger

The heat was unforgiving. The sun bared down on his shoulders like an inferno as if the Earth opened its bowels and hell ravaged the living, his hat his only respite. Cody West was a silent man who didn't have patience for the lawless behavior of the renegade gangs that spread across the land—resulting aftermath of the Civil War. Innocence had no meaning, only vengeance, and blood was free and plentiful.

Blu was Cody's war horse. The two had been together for the last five years. He was riding Blu slowly on the shadow creek trail when he heard a young woman cry out in terror. He saw the knife glimmer in the heat waves and set into a charging gallop across the creek. He headed straight for the three scumbags, pulled his pistol, and shot them dead. She was slumped down in the blood-stained creek. The "gunslinger" jumped off his horse, reached for the injured lady, and pulled her from the water. She was bleeding from a knife wound in her waist. Cody knew she needed immediate medical attention. He gently lifted her onto Blu and sped into the nearby town. The sign out front read Dr. Patterson's office; Cody charged in with the young woman limp in his arms. He carried her to the doctor's table where he gently laid her down. She was unconscious when the doctor walked in. "What happened?" the doctor asked.

"She has a knife wound," Cody replied.

"Take care of her," Cody stated as he walked out the door. He didn't notice her blood had soiled his clothes. The ruckus in the street wasn't a concern at the time. A local farmer discovered the three bodies floating in Shadow Creek. Unknowingly, his eldest daughter was the victim of an earlier attack by the three dead strangers. Cody mounted Blu and rode out of town without concern. Suspicious onlookers noticed his bloodstained clothes and the rumors spread like wildfire in a dried-up crop. It wasn't long before the ensuing posse gave chase to the tired "gunslinger." He could see a dozen riders mount the horizon behind him in a full sprint. There was no question they were coming for him. Maybe they thought he stabbed the girl. Back at the doctor's office, the young farmer's daughter awoke and grasped the doctor's hand firmly as if the thundering hooves reached back to her soul. She pulled him close and whispered in his ear; his face darkened. He left in a hurry; time was not on his side. The doctor sped outside, leaped on his horse, and headed after the posse so fast that onlookers could only stare in confusion.

Cody pulled Blu around, making him stand inside a small gorge. The sheriff hollered out to Cody to give himself up and surrender. There was a long silence. Meanwhile, the posse spread along the hill line and took cover, waiting for the word to open fire. Cody was boxed in and out of time. It was all too familiar; Cody had been in similar situations. He knew he was innocent, but it didn't matter. In times like this, you must go for it! Cody kicked his heels into Blu and said, "C'mon on, boy, let's go." He charged the firing line showing no fear of dying. With a pistol in one hand and a shotgun in the other, Cody made his stand. The roar of gunfire was deafening, as he raced toward the posse. Suddenly, the world became silent, as if life had slowed before him. He flew off his horse and hit the ground with a hard thud. As he tipped his head back and looked up to the sky, the emerging light drew him in. He thought to himself, *I'm dying.*

Hours had passed and Cody was still unconscious. Words of an angel crept into his consciousness. He thought, nothing made sense, "I must be in heaven." As his eyes slowly opened, he felt a familiar presence. He was in this same room not too long ago. A young woman entered the room with bandages covering a wound around her waist. Looking down at Cody, she said, "Thank you, you saved my life." As he looked around the room, he saw the doctor, the marshal, and the girl's father at the foot of the bed. The marshal looked down at Cody and said, "It's a brave thing you did, you saved the farmer's daughter from those three outlaws. "Gunslinger," "this time, we'll set you free!"

CHAPTER TWO
Lone Gun

The Midwest is alive, and hell rots in its deathly chains bound to consume the living, daring life with visions of peaceful mirages. And the trap is set! The will of those who walk the precipice of life and death balanced on a razor's edge. Whose soul has lost its home, death is too easy, and life is

numb with no care. Seeing a dusty old town awakens the vulnerable need for rest, a meal, some whisky, and a bed.

Blu could tell they were nearing an end to the long journey as they approached the local stables. The sunburnt barn was a reminder that hell scorched the land, and the sun was its inferno!

The hostler took Blu from Cody, and he headed to the saloon for a drink. The dusty old town was barren, and the townsfolk had abandoned the streets. The silence was almost too quiet and quieter when Cody walked across the creaky wooden deck and pushed through the squeaky saloon doors. Surprisingly, the decrepit place had many guests. Most looked like wanderers and outlaws; Cody felt at home.

The whisky burned on its way down; a few more rounds and he would be off to get a meal. He tossed six bits on the bar and walked toward the saloon door. He sensed every movement in the room as he reached the exit way. Cody had a keen awareness of the overly confident type, his hand gently resting on his pistol grip as he left the saloon. The gunslinger had a natural talent for guns and sheer luck. The few that knew him claimed he made a deal with Death. Death was happy and rich with pathetic souls. A collection of souls worthy of the devil himself. Cody's contract with Death was signed in blood. And Death consumed the abundant spoils from Cody's bullet and blade.

At the supper house, the meal was less satisfying than this place and served as a reminder that he was only passing through, riding out in the morning. Cody got up, left two bits on the table, and walked to his room. There was a knock on his door. A mild-looking hotel servant entered to prepare his bath. Steam escaped the bucket in a plume of rolling mist when the hotel servant poured the hot water into the tub. Cody asked her to leave, removed his clothes, and stepped into the warm water. He dipped his head as he laid back against the old tub. The steaming water helped him relax, but his pistol was always close. As the sun went down, Cody's eyelids became heavy as they slowly closed. His mind began drifting, as he felt the walls closing in around him. He heard the echoing cries of the dying calling to him from the past. His lost soul drowning in sin because his memories were forever branded with guilt. Sleep was a disease conjuring dreams, lies, and deceit except for one dream, the dream of his mother. She died from sickness when he was a young boy. Only in the rarest of dreams did she appear like an angel and comforted what was left of his soul.

Mornings rarely came easy. The sun peering through the window warmed his face. A bed was a rare comfort for a gunslinger. So, he took advantage of the slow awakening in this quiet moment where time stood still. Cody left the hotel and crossed the dried-up road heading for the saloon. "Give me a whisky," he said in a low, gritty voice . . . the bartender obliged. He left the bottle and walked to the other end of the bar. The saloon mirror was a welcome friend in a dried-up old town. Cody saw the shady cowboy approaching him from behind. He quickly spun with both guns pulled and caught the bushwhacker with his hand on his pistol. The place froze! Sweat poured from the cowboy's face. Outgunned, his life teetered on the edge of desperation. *This scum dog isn't worth a bullet*, Cody thought as he stared at the cowardly man. "You can call the gravedigger; he'll bury you tonight. The choice is yours!" The cowboy turned and rushed to the exit and pushed through the swinging doors so fast that they hit him in the backside as he left the saloon. It had been nearly a month since Cody enjoyed some whisky.

The day was nearing noon when the sheriff and four deputies entered the saloon and sat at a corner table. They seemed riled up about something. The sheriff spoke to them demandingly as if to forewarn the disdained audience of his dominance. Cody wasn't interested or threatened. No man bleeds any different than the other. The four deputies left the saloon in a hurry, and the sheriff yelled at the bartender to bring him a bottle. Cody's mind was on Blu. When suddenly, he heard the roar of a stagecoach approaching the town. The four horses were at full gallop, and the ground shook like an earthquake as they came to a halt alongside the hotel entrance. He wasn't paying much attention; it just happened to be the most excitement he'd seen since he arrived in this shithole. He walked out to the saloon entrance and looked across the street. He could see three ladies dressed in fancy clothes step off the stagecoach and head into the hotel. *The sophisticated type*, he thought to himself. And then it happened! A shot rang out. Cody drew his guns as the stagecoach driver fell to the ground. He could hear the woman scream from the distant hotel entrance. As if in slow motion, he sprinted across the road, firing rounds at the shooter, dropping him to the ground; Death was eager to collect his prize. Cody quickly took cover behind a barrel in front of the local store. His mind was quiet and still. A barrage of gunfire whirled past his direction. He quickly spotted the other three shooters, and his instincts took over. He pulled both guns and fired toward the water trough taking out the second gunman. In a sprint, he re-positioned himself behind a buckboard wagon. He could hear one of the gunmen running across the storefront deck, firing rounds toward him. Without hesitation, he pulled his sawed-off shotgun, stepped out, and blew two holes through the outlaw. The man dropped to his knees and fell face down, twitching as Death hovered over him, waiting for his reward. Cody rolled onto a storefront window entrance. The fourth shooter was timid and fired random shots toward him, striking the window next to him and shattering the glass. A bullet nearly grazed him, and that made him angry. He quickly reloaded both guns, stepped out onto the deck, and unleashed a barrage of gunfire hell on the fourth shooter, dropping him in front of the hotel floor. And Death smiled upon his wretched soul!

A long moment of silence hovered over the town, then the townsfolk slowly emerged from the confines of their shelter. Cody checked the dead outlaws and recognized them as the men from the saloon talking with the sheriff. These were his crooked deputies; now it made sense. The sheriff wore the devil's crown. He was terrorizing the locals and stealing all their money. The banker approached Cody and said, "I'm not sure what to say, mister. The people here are in debt to you, this money is all we have, and the sheriff and his boys just as soon kill us all and take everything we own! I must warn you; the sheriff isn't going to like this. He's coming for you." Cody ignored the banker and tipped his hat to the pretty lady in the white gown and said, "Ma'am." Then Cody turned his attention to the approaching sheriff. He looked uneasy and cross. He had his hand on his holster and stopped about six feet in front of Cody. Sheriff asked, "You shoot my men?"

Cody replied, "I did."

The sheriff said, "Drop your guns; you're coming with me. I'm taking you to jail." Cody squared up with the sheriff and rested his hands on his gun. He looked at the Sheriff and said, "No, I reckon not. I know what's going on here, Sheriff, and I don't like it. I say we finish this here and now!" The focus in Cody's eyes was as sure as a royal flush. Townsfolk started to back away; they sensed the tension between them both. From behind, Cody heard a woman shout out, "Stop." Another woman said, "Cheryl Lynn, get back here."

"Stop right now," said Cheryl Lynn as she walked between the two men. The sheriff slowly backed away, pointing his finger at Cody, and said, "Tomorrow noon, boy! You're a dead man!" Cheryl Lynn turned and looked at Cody and said, "You don't have to do this. You can leave." "The sheriff is an evil man. You're going to get yourself killed!" Cody almost smiled when he saw her pretty eyes and the look of concern on her face. She noticed his shy look of interest and felt flattered but held back, not revealing any sign of admiration. She noticed he was a gentle, handsome man. The gunslinger's confidence was sure and steady. Cody looked up at Cheryl Lynn and said, "Ma'am, I ain't afraid of the sheriff, and I never run from a gunfight!"

CHAPTER THREE

Showdown with the Sheriff

Coffins were made to order, and business in these parts was often uneventful. Today, it was a busy day for Death. The local undertaker had his work cut out for him filling four orders with a fifth underway. Who would occupy this coffin? Its rightful owner is yet to be determined. But Death will reap the reward of a fifth soul tomorrow. As the looming showdown between the sheriff and Cody West hinged on the delusions of the sheriff and his devil's crown. And the reality of a gunslinger calling.

The townsfolk were nervous with anticipation and hopeful their new guest would end the sheriff's tortuous abuse and the heinous crimes he bestowed upon them.

Sundown: Cody lay in his bed. He wasn't worried or nervous. All he thought about was Cheryl Lynn. Surprisingly, he didn't think about women much. When the war ended, life was nothing more than a day-to-day struggle to survive. He often wondered if the war had really ended; for many, it had just begun. As the sun went down, his mind drifted again, the walls were closing in, and he could hear the cries of the dying within. As the ghosts from his past crept into his consciousness, visions of Cheryl Lynn cast them aside. He drifted into his dreams. This time, instead of his mother, Cheryl Lynn appeared. She reached out and took his hand, and he faded into a deep sleep!

Meanwhile, back at the saloon, the sheriff was plotting his revenge against Cody and the townsfolk. Overly confident with his gunfighting skills, he never considered that the reserved-spoken gunslinger was quicker than him. After killing Cody, he plotted to kill the banker and Cheryl Lynn to make examples of them in front of the town. The devil's venom raced through his veins as his anger boiled within. He didn't notice Death smiling down on him, lingering over the sheriff with eager anticipation to collect his next reward.

Morning came quickly, as always. For Cody, this morning was tranquil. He didn't dwell on the unfolding events. It never crossed his mind because he wasn't thinking about the sheriff. He took his time, got up, and cleaned himself up before walking to the saloon. The streets were quiet and lonely. Only the wind blew as the sun began its daily torment. Dust whirled from the dried-up streets; and from a distance, he heard Blu call out in a snarl. He hadn't seen his horse in two days and missed his friend. *Soon, buddy*, he thought to himself as he entered the saloon. Cheryl Lynn watched Cody walk to the saloon from her hotel room window. Her mind was on him; she didn't understand what it was about him. She couldn't remember ever feeling this way with any other man. *Indeed, love doesn't happen like this*, she thought to herself. She was confused about her emotions and had a hard time containing her feelings. She felt angry at the man she had barely met. *He's too stubborn to listen to reason and he's going to get himself killed*, she thought to herself. She grappled with her internal conversation trying to understand why she was feeling this way. *Hell*, she thought, *I just met the guy!* She tried to make sense of her emotions and internalize her feelings when she noticed the locket her mother gave her as a gift. Inside was a picture of her mother and father. Then it hit her, she sat down on the edge of the bed and mumbled to herself, "I think I'm in love with a gunslinger."

At the saloon, Cody finished his whisky. The faint church bell rang out in the distance. This was his cue to make his way toward the saloon sidewalk. The squeaky bar doors rocked back and forth before finally stopping. Cody looked down the street toward the old church. There, he saw the sheriff standing in the middle of the dirt street with his hands by his side. He looked anxious, but it didn't bother Cody. He knew the sheriff was no match for him as he started walking to the street. Cheryl Lynn watched from her window with nervous anticipation. Cody was making his way toward the sheriff as the old church bell continued to ring out. She wanted to run down and tell him how she felt but knew better and didn't want to cause a distraction. She couldn't bear the thought of watching him die! "You came to the wrong town, boy," the sheriff lashed out. "You should have kept going. This is my town, and no drifter is going to kill my men and get away with it!"

Cody stopped just shy of twenty feet from the mean law dog. Time stood still momentarily as both men stared at each other, waiting for the last bell toll to ring out. The tension was quiet and still, as Cody watched the sheriff with cold intention. Suddenly, the sheriff reached for his gun but he wasn't quick enough. Cody put two rounds in his heart before the Sheriff's gun left the holster. Death applauded the sheriff's quick demise as he fell to the ground. Death snatched his soul before the devil had time to reclaim his dead apprentice! Cheryl Lynn felt relieved. It took a while before she regained her composure. She never noticed Cody walking toward the stables. The townsfolk gathered around the dead lawman and watched the undertaker collect the rightful occupant for his remaining coffin.

The hostler handed Blu's reins to Cody, as he walked outside. He wondered if he should say goodbye to Cheryl Lynn, but thought, *a woman like her doesn't want a man like me*! He climbed on Blu and said, "C'mon on, boy," and they rode out of town toward the great plains! Cheryl Lynn watched from a distance. Her heart was heavy with mixed emotions, and she wondered if she would ever see her gunslinger again. Her mind was on her trip to Idaho. She was leaving in the morning and knew it would be a long grueling journey across the great plains. She walked into the hotel and felt something. Was it Déjà vu? Intuition, or just a feeling? It didn't matter; she smiled and walked up to her room. As Cody and Blu crossed the ridge, in the distance behind them, the sun began to settle. Death followed close behind with a pouting smirk, impatiently waiting for more compensation!

CHAPTER FOUR
Blackred

Coffeeloaf

I believe animals go straight to heaven when they die. Hell exists for humankind—a place for the wretched to suffer in sin, fire, and pain. Sometimes I wonder if life and hell are the same. Animals know nothing of our pathetic existence. All they know is life and instincts until the fire burns out and the Earth reclaims the energy it gives.

Cody lifted Blu's head onto his lap, and his eyes pierced Cody's soul. "Whoa, boy, just relax." He gently caressed the side of Blu's head. Cody knew his friend was on his last breath. "I remember a young, strong horse in the fields of Tennessee," Cody said, "the bravest horse I ever saw. It's been one heck of a journey, old boy, hasn't it?" He looked down at Blu and he snorted, then lifted his head just a bit. "Shhh, it's ok, boy, I gotcha." Blu looked up at Cody. A tear formed in Blu's eye as the final breath left his body. Cody continued telling stories to his dear friend for the next few hours. Blu was gone! Cody looked around and noticed it was a beautiful location and decided to bury him where he lay. He looked for a large stone and found the perfect size and shape, then placed it on the grave. He always considered Blu his rock! He hadn't thought about it much but found himself in a situation. Out here in the middle of nowhere, miles from civilization thinking, *This is about as vulnerable as it gets. Here I am out here in the wild west, with few supplies and a horseless saddle.*

For the next few days, Cody built himself a makeshift shelter from a rock overhang on the side of a hill. He didn't seem to mind that he was in the middle of nowhere with limited supplies. He grew up living off the land. This area had plenty of wild game and fish. And plenty of water from the nearby stream. It reminded him of when he was a kid growing up in the South. Occasionally, the native hunting party rode by in the distance, but he was keen on blending in and making his presents unnoticeable. The stream ran through the forest, and on the other side was the entrance to the open plains—miles of rolling hills with large swooping valleys with the forest bordering the edge of the mountains. The cold water felt good on his face. Cody found a small quiet pool where the stream settled into a modest trickle. He dipped his head and sat in the water until it reached his waist. He laid back and relaxed in the cool water. The peaceful tranquility of his surroundings took his mind off life! Splash, splash, splash . . . Cody froze! One by one, they stepped into the water. Cody lay in the stream unnoticed as he gazed upon the most majestic view he had ever seen. There were plenty of stories about the wild horses of the great plains, but never in his life had he thought that he would be so close to such a beautiful sight. And here they were just inches from his feet. A herd of thirty-plus wild Mustangs gathered to drink from the stream he was soaking. Cody didn't move, he lay silent in the cool water, staring at the beautiful creatures. *I don't reckon I have ever seen such beauty*, he thought. Just then, a handsome stallion lowered his head and began to sip water just inches from Cody's side. As he watched the horse drink, this animal's size and strength were unlike any horse he had ever seen. His coat was black but shimmered red. He was lean and muscular like a fighter and had at least sixteen hands if not more in size. As the rest of the horses traveled downstream, this one stopped, turned, and looked Cody straight in the eyes. It didn't bother him that Cody was lying in the water watching him. The two looked at each other for a moment, then the horse turned and walked away, toward the rest of the herd. Cody lay in the stream until the horses disappeared into the forest. He got out of the water and walked back to his camp. He kept his fire small as evening settled in. He couldn't take his mind off the stallion he saw at the creek. He wondered if the herd frequently went to this place to water and get out of the sun; they might even bed down nearby in the forest.

Over the next few weeks, Cody frequented the watering hole and slowly made his presence known to the horses. They didn't seem to mind him being there. The black and red stallion always came closer to Cody as if he was not concerned at all. After several weeks of hanging out at the water hole with the wild Mustangs, Cody stood in the middle of the stream with a hand full of wild grass. The black and red stallion approached him slowly and then began eating from his hand. Cody reached out with his left hand and gently touched the stallion's forehead above his eyes. The horse didn't mind, and Cody thought, *I wonder if he'll let me ride him.* For the next few weeks, Cody attempted to mount the black and red stallion but found himself butt-first in the dirt. Cody ached from the physical pain. After his last attempt, he hobbled off to his small solitary camp. He was about to reach the clearing when a large black bear stood up on his hind legs just in front of him. He fell back and realized his gun had fallen out of the holster. Cody, in desperation, tried to move back real slow. But the bear looked ferocious and was about to charge. His teeth snarled as he let out a roar. Cody felt helpless as the bear lunged toward him. Death didn't whence. He wasn't interested in the gunslinger's soul. Out of nowhere, the front hooves from the black and red stallion cracked the bear in the skull as he yelped, turned, and stood again on his hind legs with a roar. The black and red stallion reared up and kicked the bear repeatedly. He continued to rear up, snorting and squealing as his hooves pounded the bear until the bear turned and ran away. Cody was lying on the ground in disbelief as the stallion's head bobbed up and down while snorting until he settled with a quiet nicker. Cody stood up and slowly approached the stallion who seemed to be on edge and rested his hand on his forehead. The black and red stallion lightly snorted and snarled again, "Shhh," Cody said as he gently caressed his neck. "It's ok, boy," Cody said. This moment forged a bond between the stallion and the gunslinger that would last for the rest of their lives.

It wasn't long before Cody had a saddle on his newfound friend. But he paid dearly for his efforts as he found out that this horse was as stubborn as he was and had the bruises to prove it. Their friendship was a match made in heaven. This horse was something special. Every time the gunslinger looked at him, he could tell the horse had the heart of a warrior. Cody packed the camp. It was time to get back on the trail.

Admiring the stallion, he rubbed the side of his face, looked him in the eyes, and said, "Blackred. That's what I'm gonna call you!"

Months later, riding along the outlaw trail toward Buffalo, Wyoming, Cody saw a band of Cherokee heading in their direction in a gallop. Blackred suddenly reared up and charged the oncoming gang. His sheer speed and size were so majestic that the riders splintered off the trail and scattered without any shots fired. This horse was something else, he loved a challenge. When they arrived in Buffalo and rode through town, the people stared in awe. They had never seen a horse like Blackred; so lean and muscular. You could tell by the look in this horse's eyes when they were on the trail—he loved chasing down those bad guys and sending them straight to hell!

CHAPTER FIVE
Cheryl Lynn

Fort McKinney, Wyoming.

    Cody had no interest in taking land from the natives. As far as he was concerned, this was their home long before the military and prospectors arrived. The ensuing battles took the lives of many on both sides. Gold from the black hills and deadwood gulch lured hordes of feverous fortune seekers. The infestation ignited tension between the tribes men and the intruders. Blood filled the waters, and Death welcomed the slaughter.

Cody was collecting supplies and overheard a familiar voice across the main road from the general store. "Ma'am," the sergeant replied, "you can't go north. It's too dangerous. You have to turn back." Cheryl Lynn sat on her luggage with a desperate sigh, mumbling, "What am I going to do now?" A shadow cast over her. She tried to look up, but the sun was blinding. She sensed a male figure but couldn't make out who she was looking at. She tried to use her hand to shield her eyes from the sun, but when she leaned back, her suitcase fell from under her, causing her to fall backward. The man quickly grabbed her arms to keep her from hitting the ground. He pulled her to her feet, and that's when she recognized him. "Ma'am, are you ok?" Cody asked. With a displeasing glance, she looked away momentarily, looked down at her dress, and brushed the wrinkles out with her hands while Cody watched her. He could sense her frustration but was unclear if her unenthusiastic behavior was his doing or due to her current predicament, or both. He certainly knew little of the emotions of a woman. "What brings you to this area, Ma'am?" Cody asked with a caring voice. She looked up at him and asked, "Why do you care? What's the difference between this place and the last place? You didn't seem so concerned when you rode out of town the last time I saw you." Cody looked at her in silence. He didn't know how to tell her because he started losing focus. Cheryl Lynn was the most beautiful woman he had ever seen, with her beautiful smile, the look in her eyes, and her long golden hair swaying in the wind. He was at a loss for words. When she looked at him, she realized he was admiring her with a bashful look. "I'm heading to Idaho," she said. "I'm on my way to visit my auntie in Lemhi. They are building a school for the children. I've accepted a teaching position there." Cheryl Lynn said proudly. Cody looked across the street and noticed a large company of troops preparing to head north. Cody looked at Cheryl Lynn and said, "Ma'am, let's get out of the sun." He reached down, grabbed her things, and walked toward the local lodge house. She followed behind him, eager to know his intentions. When they arrived at the lodge room, he took her luggage, placed it near the bed, and turned to see her standing in the doorway. "I beg your pardon," she said sharply. "I'm not sure who you think I am . . . I don't share a room with any man, especially someone like you who doesn't have the decency to apologize for being rude!" Cody looked at her with a puzzled face and said, "My apologies." "There are no rooms available in town. If you prefer, you can sleep in a tent with all the prospectors or you can have my room tonight. You can decide. I thought you would appreciate some privacy. Besides, I don't mind sleeping with my horse in the stable." Cheryl Lynn looked at Cody and apologized. "I've had an awful time traveling to this place. Your offer is generous, and I thank you for your kindness. I'll take your room."

"There's freshwater on the window ledge if you want to clean up. I'll be back shortly; I have to get some supplies from the store across the road. I imagine you are a bit hungry. There's a small café up the road where we can get a bite to eat when I return," he said politely. The gunslinger tipped his hat, closed the door, and walked toward the general store. Two hours later, Cody knocked on the lodge house door. Cheryl Lynn opened the door dressed in a long, beautiful rose gown. She smiled at Cody and invited him in. "Ma'am," he said, "I brought you some clothes." Surprised, Cheryl Lynn cheerfully took the box to the bed and opened it revealing some lady pants, a shirt, and a hat. She looked at Cody curiously and asked, "What is this?" Cody smiled and said, "Let's talk over diner." The cafe fell silent when Cheryl Lynn walked in. She outclassed everyone in the place, including the man she came in with. Cody helped her with her chair and sat across from her, positioning himself to see everyone in the room in case trouble broke out. They ordered dinner. Cheryl Lynn finished with a warm tea. Cody leaned closer to Cheryl Lynn and told her, "Ma'am, I'm going to escort you to Idaho, but we have to leave in the morning. I hear the Army is planning an attack on the local tribes. We need to get far away from this place. The route we'll be taking will be dangerous. Still, I believe if we go south a half a day's ride and cut through the range west, we'll reach an old trail leading through the pass. That should get us to the other side of the range. From there, we'll be in native country. Still, if we travel at night, we should be able to make our way unnoticed." Cheryl Lynn was curious to know but unsure if she was excited or scared. She knew she had to get a hold of herself to reach her auntie in time for the school opening. "Why are you doing this?" she asked Cody. He smiled and said, "This is my way of apologizing. I want to help you make it to Idaho safely!" Cody didn't notice that Cheryl Lynn's heart bounced an extra beat when he said that to her.

Finished with their dinner, they casually got up and left the restaurant and he escorted her to her lodge room. "Get some rest, ma'am, I'll come before sunrise to get you." Dawn quickly approached; Cody knocked on the lodge door quietly. It was early in the morning, but to his surprise, Cheryl Lynn was waiting and ready. They walked to the stables, where Cody had packed the horses and prepared them for the journey. Cheryl Lynn looked at Blackred and said, "Oh my, aren't you a beautiful sight?" as she petted his forehead . . . he snorted and bobbed his head in admiration as he stared deep into her pretty eyes. Cody packed the other horses. There was a younger female horse for Cheryl Lynn and an older pack horse. She was amazed that Cody had everything ready for their trip. He looked at the suitcases and said, "Ma'am, you must take just what you need for this trip. I'm sorry, the rest needs to stay." Cheryl Lynn understood the seriousness of this trip, removed some necessities and a few personal trinkets, and said, "This is all I need." Cody packed her belongings and helped her on her horse. He looked up at her while she sat on her horse and said, "Ma'am, I promise I won't let anything happen to you. I will get you to Idaho safely. Your gonna have to trust me." She looked down at Cody, smiled, and spoke, "You don't have to call me ma'am. You can call me Chery Lynn!" Cody grinned, got up on Blackred, and they quietly headed south.

Cody was alert and scanned the trail as they made their way to the south trail. He thought Cheryl Lynn would need rest soon but wanted to wait until they found good cover. There was a small opening at the forest's edge where Cody led the other horses. "Whoa, boy." Cody got off Blackred, walked over to Cheryl Lynn, and helped her off her horse. "We'll rest here for a bit." She didn't say it, but her bottom side was sore, and she moved slowly once on her feet. Cody noticed and smiled. "It'll get better in a few days," he said. Then suddenly, "Shhh." Cody gestured quietly with his finger over his lips. He quickly grabbed the horses and whispered to Cheryl Lynn, "C'mon," as they hid behind a group of trees. In the distance, out in the clearing, a group of natives passed them. Cody and Cheryl Lynn were well out of sight, but they waited a while before moving to another location, a little more secluded and deeper in the forest. After a short rest, the two traveled through the forest trail until they crossed the first mountain valley. Cody found a small hideaway to stop and rest. Cheryl Lynn looked exhausted. Cody helped her off her horse and made a bed for her. Cheryl Lynn gazed at the majestic scenery and said, "It's so beautiful here." The gunslinger brought her some hardtack and a biscuit. "Yes, Ma'am, it is," as he handed her the food. Cody walked to the shade and rested under a large pine tree near her with his rifle in his hand. They both fell into a deep sleep.

Blackred snorted and nickered, causing Cody to open his eyes. He got up and walked out to scout the area. On his return, Cheryl Lynn had packed the horses and was ready to go. He mounted Blackred turned and looked at Cheryl Lynn and asked, "Are you ready?"

She replied, "Ready!" He looked ahead and said, "C'mon, boy," as Blackred led the way through the mountain trail. The two made their way across Wyoming, traveling by night and being careful not to cause any attention. They were deep in Indian territory and had to blend in with nature as best as possible. On the tenth day, the sun began to rise when they came to a ravine. They found a spot to set up camp. Cheryl Lynn tied up the horses and took over camp duties while Cody scouted the area on foot. He made his way to a gorge that led to a river. Suddenly, the sound of many riders galloping toward him caught him off guard, so he quickly hid under the thick foliage. He peered through the bushes and saw a large native village near the riverbank. A band of native warriors was heading to their village. He also noticed on the other side of the river in a clearing, another village. This was a dangerous place to be, but Cody knew he had to get Cheryl Lynn through this, and he knew just what to do!

Cody made his way back to camp and explained the situation to Cheryl Lynn, "What are we going to do?" she asked. "Can you swim?" Cody asked. He assured her that horses were good swimmers. " At nightfall, we'll take them downstream about a half mile before we cross to the other side. We should be far enough out of sight by then to cut across the valley. Think you can do that?" He asked. "All you got to do is hang on to the saddle. Blackred and I will guide you and the pack horse along. I will tie a rope to the other horses and tie you to your harness." Cheryl Lynn was getting used to the dangerous adventure and trusted Cody's instincts. They were like a team on a dangerous mission. Nightfall, when the sun went down, the sound of celebration echoed from native villages. Wolf cries and howling chants filled the air as the warriors danced around the blazing bonfires. They were unaware of these two inconspicuous trespassers. Cody used a long rope to tie Cheryl Lynn's horse to Blackred's saddle horn. Then tied the pack horse behind them. He wrapped a rope around Cheryl Lynn's waist and tied it to her saddle. "I think this will do," he said. He looked at Cheryl Lynn and whispered to her. "Do you trust me?" She nodded her head. "Ok, real quiet and slow," he said as they entered the cool water. Hidden by the dark of night and a blanket of clouds covering the naked moon, they walked into the river where the swift water started to carry them downstream. The current was slow but steady. Cody knew Blackred was a skilled swimmer and trusted he would lead them safely down the river. "You ok, Cheryl Lynn?" Cody asked as they floated downstream with the horses . . . "I'm doing ok," she replied. "How much further until we cross over?" she asked. "Just up ahead as the river cuts around the forest. C'mon, boy," he called Blackred. They were well past any danger and had drifted in the river for a long distance. Cody tugged on Blackred to change their angle and started cutting across the river. The current began to pick up, and Cheryl Lynn found herself caught in the current pulled past the rest of the group. "Cody," she cried out. He looked over and saw her swiftly moving past her horse. Cheryl Lynn gripped the rope and wrapped it around her arm. The current pulled her rope so tight that she sunk under the water. She took a deep breath each time she went under, desperately trying to keep her head above water, but the current was strong and swift. "Hang on," Cody yelled out. "We are almost there. Let's go, boy . . . C'mon . . . haw." The water level was getting shallower as Blackred dug into the riverbed below and pulled the team closer to shore. Cody felt the rock bed below and then rushed to help Cheryl Lynn. He grabbed her rope and started pulling her toward him. He grabbed her wet shirt and said, "I gotcha." He reached down, grabbed her arm, dragged her to his side, and staggered to the river's edge where they fell to the ground. The two lay soaking wet, their arms wrapped around each other, while they caught their breath.

Tired and speechless, they looked at each other and quietly laughed at this moment of surreal comfort. Three days later, they crossed into Idaho. It was a welcome relief that they made it this far. Cheryl Lynn didn't consider Cody as a stranger or a gunman anymore. She knew he was a good man, the bravest person she had ever met. And even though she didn't know much about him, it didn't matter to her anymore. With each passing day, the journey ahead became less dangerous. Cody watched this sophisticated schoolteacher become a frontierswoman. She wasn't timid or afraid . . . this lady is a fighter. She was so beautiful; the Earth lit up beneath her. He wondered if he was good enough for a woman like her. She didn't know much about his past or the burden he had borne on his shoulders. But he knew he had feelings for her and when the time was right, he would tell her.

It was early morning. Cody awoke to the smell of freshly cooked breakfast and coffee. He watched Cheryl Lynn work on the campfire and cook as he lay in his bedroll. He never had feelings for a woman before, but he knew this was different. She brought him a plate and said, "Thought it was my turn." It was a welcome surprise. He reached out with his hand and touched her face. Cheryl Lynn grabbed his hand and pressed it against her soft cheek and smiled. Then she leaned over, closed her eyes, and gently kissed him on the lips. He had never kissed a woman before and never knew love. The moment solidified their feelings for each other and started a new chapter for the gunslinger. It took forty-six days for Cody and Cheryl Lynn to reach Lemhi. Lemhi was home to the native reservation and gold mining. Cheryl Lynn and Cody married in a beautiful meadow. He promised Cheryl Lynn he would put his guns away for her and live a simple life. The gunslinger believed that she saved him and made him a better man!

CHAPTER SIX
Black Canyon Cave

Coffeeloaf

Time doesn't wait for us to catch up. Seasons change before we notice. Moments change quicker than the wind through the trees. Years pass like months and months like days. Five years passed in the blink of an eye, but I wouldn't change anything. I only wish I had more time with her.

I held her in my arms and stared into her eyes. The pain I cried inside, knowing her last breath was near; fever consumed her with no remorse. Cheryl Lynn looked at me and said, "Take my things to my family. Tell them I love them. Promise me to live your life for me and be the man I know you can be." I looked down at her, she smiled, then she was gone. No words can describe the pain and loss that tore through my heart. It wasn't the first time in my life I had been lost. But I never felt like death's venom gnawed on my gut and sucked me into a hole. I buried Cheryl Lynn next to her favorite peach tree. I dressed her in the rose gown she wore when we first met and found a plank of oak wood to carve an inscription that read "Cheryl Lynn: My Blossom in the Wind."

I slept by her side for several days before the weather drove me into the house. Whisky did little to change the mood. I felt like a piece of me died with her. As my eyes slowly closed, the whisky bottle fell to the floor and rolled under the table. "Cody," I heard in the distance. *Where is this place? I thought to myself. Maybe I'm dreaming? Cheryl Lynn revealed herself to me, and I cried. She reached out, took my hand, and said, "Take my things to my family. Tell them I love them. Promise me to live your life for me and be the man I know you can be. I am your blossom in the wind."* The morning sun warmed Cody's face as it peered through the kitchen window. A blue jay landed on the window seal and whistled, then flew off without a care. It was then that Cody realized he had to go. He pushed through the barn door and there stood Blackred. He looked at his old friend and said, "How about we go for a ride?" Blackred snorted and bobbed his head in delight. They rode into town and Cody noticed soldiers talking with the local men across from the general store. He overheard the man in charge say they were the Army core of engineers, and they were heading to Colorado to map the territory. He said they were hiring men to join their expedition. Cody walked across the street, approached the table, and asked, "What's the job description?" The leader looked at Cody and replied, "We are mapping the Colorado territory and need able men to help.

"How are your riding skills?" the man asked. Cody said, "I can ride." "Have you ever served in the Army?" he asked. "Yes," Cody replied. "Fought many battles, including Shiloh Tennessee." The man looked up at Cody and said, "You'll do. The pay is fifty dollars a month with a hundred-dollar bonus if you finish the work." Cody signed the book and asked, "When do we leave?" Cody returned to his home and began packing his things. The peach tree was in full bloom. Cody reached up, picked a handful of peaches, put them in his saddlebag, removed his hat, and knelt at Cheryl Lynn's resting place. He whispered, "I miss you so much, Cheryl Lynn. I took a job in Colorado, I love you." Brushing a tear from his eye, he laid a rose on the oak headstone, put his hat on, and mounted Blackred. "C'mon, boy," he said, and they rode away, and he never looked back.

Cody spent nearly two years in the Colorado range, mapping the landscape for the Army core of engineers. The job would end soon, and he planned to find Cheryl Lynn's family in Crystal Mills, Colorado. The gunslinger intended to keep his promise to her. He held her memories safe in his saddle bag. Cody and his outfit had to hunker down due to a fierce winter storm that left a thick blanket of snow across the entire Colorado range. The men set up camp in the middle of a small open field. The following morning, Cody placed the saddle on Blackred. He loaded up his things out of habit.

He called to Blackred, "Hey, boy, let's go for a ride."

Suddenly from nowhere, thunder rumbled from the forest. Startled, Cody looked around and noticed none of the men in his outfit knew the impending danger. Cody quickly grabbed his rifle from Blackred's side. Before he could fire a round, shots from a native war party whirled past him, striking some other men. Cody shot two off their horses, but the third one leaped off his horse with a tomahawk and tackled Cody. The two wrestled and rolled in the wet snow while Cody held off the young brave's attempt to kill him with the sharp weapon. He was a strong warrior and had the advantage of being over him. At the same time, Cody grabbed his hand, keeping the tomahawk inches from his face. Suddenly, Blackred's hooves cracked the warrior's skull open and killed him. Cody pushed the dead warrior off him and when he looked around, he knew the warriors outnumbered their unit. His men were unable to defend themselves and were slaughtered before him. He pulled both pistols and shot eight natives in a barrage of fire and rage. He reached for his shotgun, and a bullet struck his rib cage, knocking him to his knees. He saw a group of warriors beat and bludgeon the foreman in the distance. Cody was the only man alive. The other men were already dead. He quickly got up and climbed onto Blackred and raced to the mountainside. He heard the celebratory gunfire in the background as Blackred plowed through the snow toward the forest line. Cody looked behind him and saw many natives racing toward him, but Blackred was too fast and strong. He knew they were shooting at him; he could hear the gunfire in the distance. The two reached the edge of the forest and disappeared from their sight, but they continued to pursue him.

"Cck-cck! C'mon, boy," Cody said with a winded breath.

They came to the top of the mountain ridge and cut across to the other side. The rise was steep, but Blackred handled it with ease. They were heading down the mountain's side when they came across a ravine so fast that the two had no time to stop. Blackred lunged with all his might, and they soared majestically from one mountain edge to another, clearing eighteen feet or more to the other side. They quickly cut across the steep mountainside until the ice was too much for Blackred to walk on. Cody jumped off Blackred and pulled him between some rocks. They stayed there and rested for a while to catch their breath in the cold mountain air. Cody reloaded his guns to get ready to shoot his way out. He didn't know the war party turned back after they lost his trail at the edge of the ravine. The cold was setting in and he knew they had to keep moving. Cody and Blackred worked their way across the base of several snow-covered mountains. They continued for the next four days before arriving at the entrance to the Black Canyons. Moving across a frozen stream, Cody spotted what looked like a cave opening in the distance. It was getting dark, and he was cold, weak, and tired. He pulled his pistol and entered the cave with Blackred behind him. They entered a large hollow cavern that appeared to be the only way in or out. He put his gun away, quickly gathered wood from the frozen water banks, and started a fire. Cody lay on the cold cave floor with a grunt hoping the fire would warm his numb limbs. He had lost a lot of blood but the sound of Cheryl Lynn's voice calling out to him distracted him from the seriousness of his situation. Blackred lay next to Cody and huddled near the small fire to stay warm. Cody fell unconscious and began dreaming of the Shiloh War in Tennessee.

The overwhelming guilt he carried all these years, knowing he killed so many of his fellow brothers. And the wasted lives dying slowly on the battlefield. He felt Cheryl Lynn's spirit close to him when she whispered to him, "Bring my memories to my family." Her face appeared before him, and he felt the warmth come over him. *Surely, I'll die from my wounds.* He thought to himself. Then his hand reached out to her, and she smiled and said, "Hang on, Cody, Remember your promise." Then she faded away in the distance. Cody looked up to see the firelight dance across the ceiling and began to reflect on his life, the good men who died, and his love Cheryl Lynn. *And here I lay*, he thought, *another fork in the road . . . a day late, and a dollar short*!

CHAPTER SEVEN
Angels Whispering

I feel Death hover over me, patiently waiting for my will to succumb to the inevitable. As I fall deeper into the unknown, my mind spirals into a vacuum of uncertainty. What's left of my soul retraces the haunting sounds of war and the cries of the dying. I plead to the heavens for God to take their souls and remember the daunting look on my mother's face before she died. The last words she spoke to me still echo inside and punish my heart with pain and anguish. Just like the promise Cheryl

Lynn asked of me before she died. These swelling memories of my past are tangled in my mind like a web of emotional pity.

A small tribe of Shoshone people blended in with the forest near the entrance of the Black Canyons. They are the few remaining Shoshones to survive years of fierce fighting between the powerful Cheyenne and Apache tribes in the area. They moved west across the Gunnison River and found seclusion among the forest range near the entrance to the Black Canyons. Aiyana, kin to the great spirit chief warrior Washakie is a spirited young woman who is brave and adventurous. The spirit world guides her instincts and wisdom. She is named Aiyana by her father, which means "Eternal Blossom!" Her mother and father were killed during an attack against their tribe while trying to protect her. She fled into the forest while being chased by three young warriors. She knew the warrior men would take her as a slave, but not before having their way with her. She darted through the forest in a desperate attempt to flee but tripped on an old rotten tree log along the path. She quickly turned to see the men rapidly approaching her. Then suddenly, a fierce pack of wolves emerged from the forest attacking the three men, knocking them over, and violently ripping them to pieces. Startled and frightened, she froze and never noticed the large white female wolf sitting near her with her tiny cubs. Aiyana sat still, unsure of her fate, when the wolf pack walked past her, greeting the great white wolf. The group took turns sniffing Aiyana, and the cubs climbed on her lap with playful intentions. Soon they ran off into the woods, and Aiyana followed. It was a sign from the spirit world!

After several days of traveling, the wolf pack led her to a small remote village. She turned to the white wolf and said, "*Mukuai beya ish, aishen* (spirit wolf, thank you)! You saved my life." Five years passed since that horrific day. Aiyana awoke in the early morning from a re-occurring dream. The spirit wind called to her in the voice of an angel. She slipped through the opening of the wigwam and followed the voices through the snow-layered forest. She knew this path well. It was the path to the entrance of the Black Canyons. Native tales spoke of superstition and called the Back Canyons "much rock big water." The old stories made the Black Canyons the perfect place for the small Shoshone tribe to hide away when their enemies were dangerously close. The moon cast shadows against the forest and lit the path along the frozen creek bed. The spirit wolf watched from a distance. Aiyana could see their eyes glow from deep within the forest. She was not afraid; the spirit wolf was her guardian. They protected her while she made her way to the Black Canyons entrance. The familiar scent of firewood smoke caught her attention as the spirit wind called to her again.

Two-day-old tracks from a single horse and rider left a trail through the snow-covered riverbed that led deeper into the Black Canyons; blood stains followed. Aiyana followed the tracks with cautious curios-ity, and the scent of burnt wood became more assertive as she made her way deeper into the canyon. In the distance, she could see the faint glow of yellow light flickering from what appeared to be a receded opening to a cave. She quietly crept up to the edge of the entrance, knelt, and slowly peered around the rock entrance. There he lay. She cautiously moved closer but stayed close to the cave wall. *Who is this man?* she thought to herself. She could tell he was injured and could hear him moaning. Aiyana saw Blackred lying near the fire. He looked tired and thirsty. She slowly approached Cody, touched his forehead, and felt his fever. She opened his jacket, pushed aside the guns, and opened his blood-stained shirt to reveal a bullet wound on his upper right rib. Luckily, it was a clean shot straight through. This man endeared a lot of pain and would surely die if she left him alone. The spirit wind called out again, and Cody's hand raised as if to touch something. She could feel the strength in his heart, and her instincts took over.

Cody had cooking gear with his saddle bag. She grabbed his water pouch and poured some water into his mouth, then poured water into her hands for Blackred. He lapped it up eagerly. Aiyana left the cave quickly in search of some necessities. She knew the gifts the great spirit mother shared in abundance. When she returned to the cave, she brought a basket with firewood, herbs, cloth, clay bowls, and wood utensils. She also carried a large buffalo hide slung on her back. She made the fire burn hotter to warm the inside of the cave and melt snow for water. She boiled fresh meat and bone to make a broth, mixed herbs with peyote, and soaked the mixture in hot water. She removed Cody's clothes, washed his body with warm water, and packed his wound with herbs. Then she wrapped it with cloth and covered him with the buffalo hide. She fed him broth, then made him drink the herb peyote tea. She placed some herbs over the fire, and smoke filled the cave. Aiyana danced and sang around the fire, waving her skirt to force smoke over Cody's body. His mind slipped in and out of consciousness as pain surged through his veins. He felt his spirit rise from his body up through the cave floor. His soul drifted upward and hovered high above the canyon, facing the stars. *I must be dying*, he thought to himself.

The clouds raced across the sky, and the sun set and rose three times in what felt like a moment. The sound in the distance echoed through the canyons and whirled through his head. Then, all movement stopped, and a divine light appeared from the heavens and began to warm his face. A voice called out to him, and he felt the familiar presence of Cheryl Lynn. He raised his hand, and she appeared before him. "Cody, my love," she said and took his hand. "You must wake up. Take my things to my family. Live your life for me and be the man I know you can be." She took Cody's hand and brushed away a tear from his eye. Cody looked up at Cheryl Lynn. Her wings spanned the heavens. He couldn't speak. The overwhelming emotion he felt at that moment was pure love. As Cheryl Lynn began to fade, she whispered.

"The girl, she is the one. Love her as you love me." Suddenly, Cody felt his spirit being pulled back to Earth as he plummeted to cave below. At that moment, he took a vast surging breath. His eyes opened as his lungs filled with air. He looked around the cave and saw Aiyana's shadow dancing in the firelight across the cave wall. It was such a surreal moment. He had to take a minute to regain his thoughts. The gunslinger tried to get a grip on his situation. He looked over and saw Blackred watching him as he snorted. Cody's awareness was returning, but he felt exhausted and fell into a deep sleep. As he drifted into his dream, the vivid reminder of Shiloh gripped his soul, and hell opened the gates to reveal fire and death as the lost souls of the innocent cried out in pain.

CHAPTER EIGHT
The Silence Is Killing Me

Cody lay on the cave floor feverish. Aiyana continued to care for him and fed him the medicinal mixture of herbs and peyote. His eyes rolled back into his head as he drifted to another place in time. The Shiloh War! They were young, their eyes silent and still, hollow in death. Their cries for help are now silenced forever, and their remains litter the fields in disbelief. Death is not partial to age but welcomes much carnage, as there is no limit to feasting fresh souls. Death is neither hungry nor full. It merely

takes what life gives.

Dreaming the aftermath:

The morning chill sank her teeth into my spine as I walked the fog-layered fields. I remember the thousands upon thousands of soldiers who lay dead. And my ears are still ringing from two days of battle and cannon fire. I choked on my breath and tried to swallow, but the taste of blood and gunpowder overwhelmed my senses. I found a broken tree limb to sit and collect myself. I wiped the blood from my eyes and wondered how I survived. The senseless killing brings no honor, and I struggle to understand it all. We were collecting the dead, stacking them on wagon carts to be buried in the cemetery, but time and resources left thousands disinterred where they lay. The battlefield became a grave for those whose names would be forever lost. The pain and guilt were too much for my soul. I felt a hollowness inside as it left my body. I wanted to cry, but tears would not form. There were none left to give, and I wished I had died that day.

In the Black Canyon cave:

Aiyana tried to comfort Cody as he appeared squeamish and lay in a deep sleep. She knew he was on a journey; she tossed more herbs on the fire, bellowed the smoke across his face, and began a medicine dance chanting, "*away-oh-way-a-oway, away-oh-way-a-oway*" in a soft melodic voice.

Dreaming:

Cody re-lived the two days before the Shiloh aftermath. It was unexpected, a surprise attack caught our regiment off guard. Overwhelmed with gunfire, we were forced to withdraw from our position. Lucky for us, reinforcements from behind rallied an advance. The fresh troops were welcoming, which gave our unit the courage to push back and drive forward. He remembered soldiers falling in the brush on both sides, and the forest was drenched in blood. We fought for hours before clearing the trees and entering an opening to a field. Three men stood in the distance firing at our line, taking out two men next to me, their blood splattered in my face. I rushed toward them with my bayonet and lodged it in the first man's chest as the other two tried to reload their rifles. I quickly pulled my revolver and shot the closest man in the head; he fell over stiff and toppled over an old, rotted tree trunk. Focused on the remaining soldier, I pulled my bayonet from the first man who crumbled before me. My rifle, ready with a loaded round, was aimed at the heart of the third man, quickly drawing down on me. But I was too fast; I pulled the trigger before he could position himself, and my bullet blew through his heart. *Death swooped in and collected their souls.* A fourth soldier rushed toward me, screaming like a wild man. He swung his rifle toward my head. I ducked and used his forward motion to flip him to the ground. We rolled and grappled until I took out my knife and drove it into his chest. He whimpered and coughed, then died in my hands.

It was madness, our troops finally overtook the enemy's barrage, and they passed me in a flurry, killing the rest of the pursuers. There was little time to gather my thoughts. A fellow soldier reached down and helped me to my feet . . . "Come on," he said, "we are re-grouping. There's a big enemy battalion heading toward Shiloh. Grant has positioned his troops for a forward assault."

Nothing can prepare a man for the sound of a hundred canons and thousands of rifles firing in every direction. A six-pound cannon slug would blow through a regiment at fifteen hundred yards and obliterate everything in its path.

When we arrived, the fighting had already begun. We took position along a ridge and watched in awe as the battle unfolded. I felt numb inside. Fear had long left my conscious. I knew my chances of death were the same as any man fighting that day. We fought nonstop for two days and drove what was left of the enemy into retreat. The others lay dying in the fields. They cried out in pain throughout the night, and I prayed to God, *"Take them by your side." We were brothers, sons, and fathers.*

We received word that we were moving to Corinth, Mississippi. As we marched past the Shiloh Church, the sign in front of the porch read, *"Place of Peace."* Cody recalled whispering, "Not today," as he stood looking at the sign with cold, tired eyes! Cody whimpered the words "Place of Peace," then drifted off again. Aiyana wiped his forehead with a wet cloth to cool his forehead. Aiyana cared for Cody for five days as he drifted in and out of consciousness and mumbled while dreaming as if talking to the spirit world. On the morning of the sixth day, he slowly opened his eyes and uttered, *"The silence is killing me,"* and realized that he lost his soul in the fields of Shiloh!

CHAPTER NINE
Blossom in the Wind

It's rare when two souls connect. Guided by an unforeseen force, an unexplainable coincidence brings two unsuspecting souls together at a point in time when the vulnerability is open to the spirit calling, and they become soul mates.

Aiyana fed Cody warm broth and dressed his wound. Cody's fever broke, but he continued long hours of sleep. Cheryl Lynn's spirit was close to him, and he spoke to her. "I feel you next to me," he said, "but who is this girl mending my wound and feeding me broth?" He held his hand to her face and whispered, *"The pain of losing you, a part of me wants to die too. If I let go, I'll be with you in heaven as one."* Cheryl Lynn smiled and said, "Cody, remember your promise." Then she faded away. Aiyana was standing near the cave entrance. The sunlight shone across her face, and she turned to look at him. It was that moment that Cody realized how beautiful she was. "What is your name?" Cody asked quietly. He pointed his fingers at her and said, "You name?" he tapped his chest and said, "Name, Cody," and repeated the gesture twice. She walked over, kneeled beside him, wiped her chest, and said, "Aiyana." Cody smiled and said, "Thank you I don't know who you are, but you saved me from dying here alone." He looked at her and said, "You are like a blossom in the wind." Aiyana put her fingers on his lips and said, "Shish." She put her hand to her head and motioned to imply sleep and said, *"Tatigi,"* then repeated the motion softly and said, *"Tatigi."* Cody understood what she was saying and closed his eyes. Within moments, he was drifting into a deep sleep! Blackred and Aiyana formed a friendship over the next few weeks as she cared for Cody and nursed Blackred back into shape. *"An-ke-pom-py,"* she called Blackred, which meant "Red Hair." She was impressed by his size and strength and frequently rode him to gather food, water, and supplies. She returned one afternoon with a small deer slung over Blackred's back. She was a skilled hunter, as she should be. Her family were fierce hunters and warriors. Cody was surprised to see the friendship develop between Aiyana and Blackred. His recovery had taken more than eight weeks, and he knew that he and Blackred would not have survived without her help. The two enjoyed the fresh deer meat she prepared over the fire. Afterward, they taught each other words in English and Shoshone language.

"My family once lived in all the land, we were great warriors, descendants of the great spirit chief Washakie," she said. She told Cody how many of her people died in battle fighting neighboring tribes. The women and children were taken and enslaved and never seen again. She explained to Cody how her mother and father sacrificed their lives to save her and how the great white spirit wolf led her to the small tribe she now called home. She explained to Cody the night the spirit wind called her and led her to him. The voice of someone he once loved called her in the night. When she saw the glow from the firelight, she knew it was a sign from the heavens. "When I found you," she said, "the death spirit was hovering over you, waiting for you to cross over. I banished Death from the cave with the sacred healing dance." Cody looked at Aiyanna as she told her story and realized something more was happening here that he couldn't explain. "My parents named me Aiyana. In Shoshone, it means "Eternal Blossom." She looked at Cody and said, "I am the Blossom in the Wind!" At that moment, Cody's mind was taken aback. How could this be? He barely knew this woman. He always called Cheryl Lynn his blossom in the wind. He recalled the dream he had when Cheryl Lynn came down as an angel and told him, "The girl, she is the one, love her as you love me." He realized Cheryl Lynn's spirit all along brought the two together.

Mid-afternoon spring:

The snow had melted, and the canyon stream flowed again, becoming a river. New life sprung from the rich soil, and the great mother displayed her beauty as the sun lit the canyon walls and revealed layers of spectacular color.

Cody, now fully healed from his wounds, spent his days learning the ways of the Shoshone as he and Aiyana grew closer together. Well hidden from the outside world, life in the Black Canyon cave was simple, and no other care existed. Cody was fishing when the wolf pack surrounded him. He felt helpless and vulnerable. The white wolf approached him with a snarl, then Aiyana appeared. She knelt beside the white wolf and said, "*Mukuai Beya ish* (spirit wolf). Something is not right." Suddenly, the wolf pack quickly ran away. Aiyana looked at Cody and said, "We must take shelter." Fortunately, the fire was not burning, so there was no smoke from the cold ashes. Cody and Aiyana watched from the shadows as a pack of neighboring native warriors slowly rode across the upper ledge of the canyon. She knew they wouldn't enter the canyon because of fear and superstition. Aiyana feared they were heading toward her village. There were at least twenty riders. Aiyana looked at Cody and said, "We must warn my people."

They quickly gathered their weapons and jumped on Blackred and raced towards Aiyana's village. They arrived at the canyon entrance and started down the secret trail that led to her village. Blackred was sprinting through the forest in a blazing gallop. The spirit wolf and her pack were behind her as they approached her village. Aiyana hollered out the traditional "*A-yi-wa, A-yi-wa*" danger call and shouted, "*Ya-ma-sua, yama-sua*" (hurry up, hurry up). The people from her village began scurrying about in preparation for an attack. The men grabbed their weapons and took a position. The woman rushed the children off and hid deep in the forest. The Shoshone men didn't notice Cody and Blackred with Aiyana. Their focus was on the imminent attack. They were well prepared and hidden from their enemy, who no longer possessed the element of surprise. There was a long silence, then a Shoshone man made a little bird sound, warning the others that the enemy was nearby. Suddenly ten warriors on foot began rushing through the forest toward the village, yelling in high pitch battle cry. They carried their hand weapons openly and dashed in a full sprint toward the village. Their eyes were fierce, and their faces were adorned with battle paint. Cody watched in amazement but was not afraid. He knew he could single-handedly take them out, but deep inside, he did not quarrel with either side. In an instant, six men were seized by net traps around the perimeter. The warriors were caught off guard as the nets wisped them high into the trees. The Shoshone men in hiding overcame the other four warriors; death came swiftly, and their tongues were silenced. The forest began to rumble as the roar of warriors on horseback began to get louder as they reached the edge of the woods. Two Shoshone warriors jumped out to face the oncoming attackers, but the riders were too swift. One died from a spear that punctured his chest. The other suffered a fatal blow to the head from the enemies' war club. The ten riders were now fighting with the remaining Shoshone men within the village grounds. Aiyana jumped from Blackred and ran toward the fighting, and the spirit wolf and her pack followed. An enemy horseman swinging his battle club charged toward her with deadly intentions. Cody took out his shotgun and blew him off his horse. The wolf pack attacked the remaining riders knocking them off their horses and gnawing on their limbs. The leader shot a black wolf with an arrow and started charging toward Aiyana, but Cody and Blackred were already there. Cody lunged off Blackred and tackled the leader, knocking him off his horse. They both fell to the ground, and the battle between them began. Cody, fresh from recovery, had the strength of three men. His fighting skills were unmatched. The warrior leader pulled his knife and lunged toward Cody, but Cody took control on the ground and locked him in a choke hold securing his feet. He had the blade against his attacker's throat, ready to end his life.

Unaware that they were surrounded by Aiyana and her clan, who had already secured the rest of the enemy, they were all bound and, on their knees, watching Cody and the chief warrior battle. Cody said, "*Ha li wi s ta* (stop), *Ha li wi s ta* (stop)." He squeezed tighter with his choke hold and pressed the knife against the warrior's neck until it lightly cut his skin. The warrior leader relaxed his arms, letting them lay out limp as a sign of surrender. Cody stood up and helped the man to his feet. Aiyana rushed to his side relieved and introduced Cody to her people. She explained how the spirit wind guided her to him and that it was a sign from the spirit world. Cody had learned some Shoshone language from Aiyana and spoke in broken words to both groups, "I fought in the great white man's war. I watched innocent men die and suffer on the battlefields, and I feel no honor in my actions. I have no enemies here and do not want to fight against any people. We can live peacefully and share the great mother's land together. I have walked beside death all my life. My soul has been lost in remorse. We can live in peace with these men and set them free to rejoin their families to live another day."

The Shoshone chief walked up to Cody and spoke to him, "Your spirit speaks of truth and love; war is never good and only brings death. We do not wish to battle our enemies but instead, welcome them as guests to our homes." The chief approached the warrior leader and looked him in the eye. "The white spirit has spoken," he said, "what say you and your people?" He looked around and said, "I am Chief Bear Claw. The white spirit man speaks with wisdom. His words are great medicine. I owe my life to him. The days of fighting our neighboring tribes must end. We will honor a treaty." He raised his fist in the air and shouted, "*Haw-Yaw-Yaw-Ye-Haw-Yaw-Yaw-Ye*." Then everyone joined in the customary chant.

The two groups celebrated for three days, sharing stories, and learning about Cody and Blackred. Aiyana shared her story with her people. They listened with great interest but couldn't help noticing the connection between Aiyana and Cody. The Shoshone chief stood up and asked Cody to stand. He removed the eagle claw necklace from his neck and placed it around Cody's neck. "My father gave this to me after my first hunt to symbolize becoming a man to serve our people. I pass this symbol of the eagle's free spirit to you and welcome you as a brother to our people. You are a warrior with great wisdom, honor, and bravery symbolic of the strength and power of the great eagle spirit." He then held up an eagle's feather and sang a chant. Then he said, "Father sky, welcome this man to share the creator's vision of balance between earth and the spirit world." He said to Cody, "Protect this feather. The eagle spirit will guide you safely through life and in passing." Aiyana stood up and walked over to Cody. She took the feather and began to weave it into his hair. The chief looked at Cody and said, "From this day forward, your name is White Eagle."

Aiyana was staring at Cody with much admiration. Her people had noticed how close they had become. The chief spoke to them both in front of the tribe. "The spirit wind spoke and brought these two together. White Eagle," he said, "Aiyana will be your wife. I have spoken. Cody gazed into Aiyana's eyes and spoke to her; "the great spirit brought us together." "My heart has bonded with yours." "I am honored to have you as my wife." The Chief said, "We will prepare for the ceremony."

For the next few days, the village people prepared for the wedding ceremony. The Apache warriors said goodbye to the Shoshone tribe and left in peace. The wedding ceremony was unlike anything Cody could have imagined. Blackred stood next to Aiyana. She was adorned in the finest leather outfit with hand-stitched beads and turquoise. She looked beautiful, and Cody felt his soul had been restored. He celebrated with his new wife and family for several days and enjoyed the storytelling. While sitting beside the fire alone one evening, he sensed Cheryl Lynn's spirit close to him. "I can feel you close to me," he said, "before you died, looking into your eyes the pain, I cried. The pain of losing you, a part of me surely died too. I feel you're smiling down on me. You saved me again, and I will always love you. You are my blossom in the wind."

The day came for Cody and Aiyana to leave. They said their good-byes and began their journey to Crystal Mills, Colorado. They rode off with Cheryl Lynn's memories still wrapped in the cloth she made for Cody, safely tucked away in his saddle bag. "I will fulfill my promise to you," he said to Cheryl Lynn under his breath, "and return your memories to your family." The sun slowly rose as they disappeared in the distance.

CHAPTER TEN

Bounty Man

Evil spawns its web, and the slow decay of sanity becomes entangled in a world of delusion. The mind-altering events that trigger psychopathic rage manifest into aggressive and unstable behavior. The Angel of Death devours the living to satisfy an unquenchable thirst for blood and to feast on their fear when the moment before death is inevitable. There is no recourse but to give up the soul. He is the most feared predator of man; he is the son of the devil.

A demon horse slowly walks through the streets. A shadow clouds the sun while darkness lingers over the small town. No one dares to gaze upon the man riding the dark horse. A packhorse followed close behind with three bodies slung over the horse's back, their limbs tied across the underbelly. The rider stopped at the jailhouse and climbed off his horse. Silence came over the town as he tied his horse to the hitching post. His only interest was collecting his reward and more wanted posters from the local sheriff. There was no small talk. The rider pulled three wanted posters from his long jacket and handed them to the sheriff. "Bart," said the sheriff to his deputy, "go look." Bart walked outside and looked over the three dead men. He returned and said, "Yeah, that's them." Then Bart said, "Sheriff, one of them boys have a silver spoon jammed in his eye socket." The sheriff looked at the dark rider, stood up, walked to his safe, opened it, pulled out nine thousand dollars, and handed it to the "bounty man." As the "bounty man" grabbed the money, the sheriff held onto it, gave a little tug, and said, "Mister, you ride out of this town. I don't want to see you harassing the good people here, you understand!" The "bounty man" pulled the money from the sheriff's grip, looked at him with one eye, gave him a smirky grimace, turned, and walked out. "Bart," the sheriff said, "take those men to the caretaker, and you watch that man leave my town."

"Yes, sir," Bart replied. Rumors spread across the land about a "bounty man" called the Angel of Death. His legend grew as he singlehandedly delivered more wanted men dead than any other "bounty man" in the territory. He was a dark rider with a large dark evil horse. He had a patch across one eye and a scar from his forehead across his other eye and down his face to his neck. Rumors mentioned a soldier from the civil war killing native women and children. They said seven warriors had captured him. They cut his left eye out and sliced his face across his right eye. They said he laughed at them, then ripped the throat out from one warrior and began to eat it. Startled, the remaining warriors, fearful that he was an evil spirit, tried to retreat, but he cut them all to pieces and made a monument with their limbs. When neighboring tribes found the memorial, they claimed it was the work of the "Bad God."

He was four when he witnessed his father mutilate his mother with a clever. The authorities found his father in the barn, drunk and laughing. He was hanged the next day. They said he was laughing until the rope snapped his neck. The boy was sent to an orphanage where the headmaster constantly beat him, but he never shed a tear. Five years later, they found the headmaster with a fork jammed in his aorta. The boy was missing and never seen again.

He was seventeen when he joined the Confederate Army. He killed three soldiers while they slept. He took a uniform and fought alongside a small unit of bushwhackers until they were ambushed. He survived by changing his uniform and pretending to be a Union soldier. He didn't care about north or south. The war didn't interest him. He was there for the killing. The thrill of ending life was overwhelming, and killing became his sole purpose!

After a long battle, he often walked the fields of the dying in the late evening, looking for the wounded and suffering to deliver the final blow. He used his knife to watch the victim bleed out, standing over them until life left their eyes. The Angel of Death was a hedonistic killer who sought continuous gratification to fuel his masochistic lust for death. When the war ended, his thirst for blood had become habitual. He rode alongside a group of mercenaries on a killing spree hunting down affiliates of the Confederate renegades. They slaughtered innocent wagon trail groups in small numbers for sport and to replenish their supplies. The night the mercenaries agreed to disband and go their separate ways, the Angel of Death severed their throats while they slept. The authorities assumed it was the work of the local native tribe.

The Angel of Death continued his rampage, killing natives in silent rage until he lost his eye. Wandering aimlessly in the hot sun with open wounds on his face, he came across a small homestead with a small family. They took him in and helped him heal. Once he recovered from his from his wounds, he killed the family in their sleep and burned their house to the ground. Not before taking the husband's belongings and his horse. He rode into a wicked cow town in Kansas. "Welcome to Ellsworth," the shot-up sign read. As he entered the old town, gunfire erupted in the middle of the street as the sheriff began to shoot at several outlaws. The outlaws returned fire, killing the sheriff. The Angel of Death mumbled, "Hell is my home."

He stopped at the jail and noticed large reward signs posted out front for wanted men stating, "Dead or Alive." The reward money attracted his attention. Then he turned and watched the ensuing chaos in the street. The deputy entered the jail. The dark rider sat in a chair, waiting for someone in charge. The deputy was surprised when he saw the dark rider with his scar and black patch. He was an evil sight for any man to look at. "Jesus, mister," the deputy said, startled. "What are you doing here?" The deputy asked him, then he said, "Look, I have a dead sheriff out there and a town full of outlaws. What business do you have here?"

"Any of those men have a wanted poster with a reward?" asked the Angel of Death. The deputy pulled out three wanted posters and said they were at the saloon. The Angel of Death took the posters, looked at their faces, folded them, and put them in his jacket. He walked out of the jail and down to the saloon. He pushed through the saloon doors and looked around. The place was bustling with chaotic business. He spotted the three men at a card table and grimaced. He walked up to the card table without hesitation, pulled both his stub nose and colt forty-five, and put a bullet in the head of two outlaws. He took his long knife and stuck it in the throat of the third fella. The place was silent as the Angel of Death made his presence known, and fear overcame the saloon. The deputy burst in with both guns drawn and saw the three outlaws dead on the floor. The Angel of Death pulled out the three wanted papers, looked at the deputy, and said, "You owe me four thousand dollars." The deputy looked at the dark stranger, paused momentarily to catch his breath, and said, "Who are you?" The Angel of Death looked at him and said, "I'm the Bounty Man!"

CHAPTER ELEVEN

Hell Bent on Revenge

God's land is vast, with incredible lush, colorful landscapes. To witness such beauty in the mountains of Colorado is beyond words to describe. The mountain range is a kaleidoscope of endless tapestry where the sun illuminates spectacular imagery worthy of heaven. Majestic waterfalls adorn the chiseled mountains where snow-topped peaks look like clouds where angels rest as they peer across the endless horizon. To witness Earth's seductive garden is a reminder that life is a precious balance of necessity

and to live harmoniously with mother nature. God wills us to be the keepers of heaven on Earth.

Crystal Mills would be a ten-day ride on horseback. They were in no rush. Aiyana rode by Cody's side. He felt he had been given a new beginning. They were heading to Crystal Mills, Colorado. Cheryl Lynn's family had moved to Crystal Mills when she finished boarding school. Her father worked for the silver mines and led the tunnel construction at Sheep Mountain. Cody's heart was heavy as he knew the news of their daughter's death would be heartbreaking. But his love for Cheryl Lynn was so embedded in his soul. Nothing mattered more to him than fulfilling his promises to her. On the seventh day, they made camp near a beautiful waterfall. It was the perfect spot to stop and enjoy time with Aiyana. They swam at the waterfall's base and camped near the water's edge. Cody struggled with how life here was far removed from the chaos of a gunslinger's life.

The light passed through the water mist as the sun set, creating a giant rainbow. The arch touched down in the distance toward their destination. The moon perched itself above their campsite when the sun rested for its evening. "*Baa Muh* (water moon)," Aiyana said with a smile as the full moon hovered over them and lit the waterfall . . . The sound of the rushing water was tranquil and the perfect setting for love. In the distance, the spirit wolf made her presence known with a long howling call to Aiyana. She had no fear as the two lay beside the fire, looking up at the naked sky. The spirit wolf was always close by, watching over her. After three days of riding through the majestic mountain range, Cody and Aiyana reached Crystal Mills. The small mining town was quiet, but the landscape was beholding. Cody tied Blackred to a hitching post and helped Aiyana off her horse. They knocked on the weathered door of a small cabin. The door opened, and a woman stood at the doorway and asked, "May I help you?"

Cody replied, "Yes, ma'am, I'm looking for Mr. and Mrs. Ross."

"Kate and Henry Ross," she replied. "Yes, ma'am."

"Who's asking?" she said inquisitively.

"Ma'am, my name is Cody West. I bring news of their daughter Cheryl Lynn."

"Oh my," she said, "Cheryl Lynn. All they talk about is their daughter and how beautiful she is. Is she still teaching in Idaho?"

"No, ma'am? Can you tell me where to find her parents?"

"Why sure, they live in the lodge by the creek. Look for a garden in front of their house. It must be close to supper time. Henry should be home about now." Cody tipped his hat and said "Ma'am," and they left. They walked with their horses down to the creek and found the lodge with a garden tucked nicely within the trees. The smell of supper filled the air. They tied their horses to a tree, walked to the door, and knocked. The door opened, and an astute man answered the door. "May I help you?" he asked.

"Are you Henry? Henry Ross, sir," Cody asked. In the background, a woman spoke, "Henry, who's at the door? Don't just stand there. Invite them in."

"Come in, please," he said. Cody and Aiyana entered the home, removed their jackets, and sat near the fireplace. "How can we help you, son?" he asked.

"My name is Cody, Cody West." Kate stopped and turned around. "Are you my Cheryl Lynn's Cody? I received a letter from her after you were married. Where is she? Why are you here without her?" Cody choked, and his eyes blurred as he looked at both parents. He couldn't speak. The obvious became apparent. Mrs. Ross cried out in a quiet voice, "No, no," and ran to Henry. The two embraced each other and cried. Cody approached them and said, "Fever took hold of her, and she died in my arms." Aiyana and Cody hugged the two parents as they mourned their daughter's passing. The next day, Henry approached Cody, "You are welcome to stay, you are my son-in-law, and I know you did your best to take care of my Cheryl Lynn."

"Sir, I loved Cheryl Lynn with all my heart. I think of her every day. It's taken nearly four years to make it here. It's been a hard road, and I wouldn't be here if it weren't for Aiyana." He explained to Henry about the ambush in the Colorado range and hiding in the Black Canyon cave near death. That's when Aiyana came along and helped him. Kate called everyone to dinner. The four sat at the dinner table. It was apparent that Kate was trying to change the mood but was still shaken. After dinner, Kate went straight to work cleaning the dinner table. She was trying to keep her mind off the inevitable truth that her daughter was gone, and she would never see her again.

Cody got up and walked out the door. He walked out to Blackred and gave him a pat on the forehead. Then reached down to the saddle bag lying on the ground and pulled a cloth-wrapped package stashed inside. He got up, returned to the house, and entered through the front door. Aiyana was helping Kate with the cleaning. Henry sat near the fire, quiet and mournful. "Mrs. Ross," Cody said, "Cheryl Lynn asked me to return these to you. She called them her memories." He held the cloth-wrapped bundle up, offering it to her. Henry stood up and reached for the package. Cody handed it to him gently. He walked to the table, laid it down, and began to unwrap the cloth. Kate walked over to the table and sat next to Henry. Aiyana sat next to Cody as the two parents unwrapped the leather bundle. They unfolded the cloth within and revealed four objects. The first two items unwrapped were an enchanted silver-handled mirror and a matching silver-handled brush. Kate recognized them and said, "This belonged to my mother. She gave them to me on my wedding day. I gave them to Cheryl Lynn the day she left for Idaho. The third item was a Victorian sapphire pendant brooch. "This was a gift from her grandparents when she finished boarding school," Kate said. The fourth item was a small journal. Cody said, "Cheryl Lynn wrote to you daily. She loved sharing her adventures. She was planning to give it to you in person." The inscription on the cover read, "Blossom in the Wind." Kate held the book to her chest and began to cry, muttering, "Thank you," then turned and walked to her bedroom, clutching the book against her heart. Cody told Henry he had the book made for Cheryl Lynn as a gift for her first day as a teacher. He looked at Cody, reached out his hand, and said, "Thank you," and the two men shook hands. Henry turned and said, "I'm going to check on Kate," and walked to the bedroom.

Cody and Aiyana spent two weeks visiting Henry and Kate before saying goodbye. "Where are you heading?" Henry asked. Cody replied, "Thought we would give Texas a try. Had enough of the cold weather." Kate handed Aiyana a small package. Aiyana opened it and revealed a small music box. She opened the lid. The sparkling sound played a melody, and Aiyana's face lit up. Kate smiled and said, "The song was 'The Dew is on the Blossom.' It was Cheryl Lynn's favorite song. I want you to have it." They all hugged and said their goodbyes, then Cody and Aiyana rode away, following the trail to town.

Cody and Aiyana rode north for two days, then headed east toward

Breckenridge. They camped along the blue river and enjoyed the scenic ride. Food was abundant, and Aiyana was a skilled hunter, something all Shoshone women shared. Breckenridge was a small town built by prospectors. Cody and Aiyana stopped for supplies, then kept riding. He couldn't help but notice the large number of fresh coffins being buried in the cemetery outside of town. A rickety old sign read, "Beware the Angel of Death." They rode for five days heading to Colorado Springs when they entered the garden of the Gods. The two stood and witnessed the beauty of the giant rock formations in the distance. It looked like the perfect place to set up camp for the day. Cody got off Blackred and grabbed his saddle. Aiyana was admiring him when a thunderous shot rang out from out of nowhere.

Cody quickly turned to see Aiyana drop to the ground. In horror, he rushed to her side. In the distance, a lone rider fired another shot. Cody pulled his rifle and emptied ten rounds in a barrage of long-range shots toward the shooter. He rushed to Aiyana and dragged her to his side; she was unconscious. He looked for signs of bleeding and noticed a hole in her pouch and another in the side of her breechcloth with blood oozing. He quickly opened her breechcloth to look at her wound. The bullet skimmed her waist side, leaving an open gash but nothing too serious. He grabbed the pouch, which seemed quite heavy, and opened it. He looked inside and saw the music box that Kate had given her and pulled it out. The bullet dented the front cover, and the impact had knocked her off her horse unconscious. The bullet ricocheted off the lid and just barely nicked her.

Cody laid her head on his waist and began to rub her face. "Aiyana, Aiyana," he said in a calm voice. Aiyana slowly opened her eyes, and Cody choked on a tear, then smiled and hugged her. The great white spirit wolf walked up to Aiyana and licked her face. The spirit wolf let out a series of loud howling calls. A large pack of wolves emerged from the trees and gathered around them. The white wolf looked Cody in the eyes, snarled, then let out three growling barks. Cody knew what this meant. He kissed Aiyana and said, "Stay here and wait for me."

He got up, saddled Blackred, reloaded his rifle, and headed after the shooter. The white wolf howled, and the pack raced away, following Cody. The sun was setting on the distant horizon. Cody knew he must push hard to pick up the shooter's trail. Blackred sprinted like a freight train through the mountain terrain. There was a surge of confidence in Cody. He was hell-bent on revenge, and nothing was going to stop him. Suddenly the wolf pack veered rapidly to the left. They started barking as they raced toward a series of giant rock formations. A shot rang out at Cody, and he missed. Cody saw the location of the shooter. They cut back behind the rocks, found an opening to cross through, and found the shooter surrounded by the wolf pack. His horse kept rearing up, making shooting at the wolves difficult for the shooter. Cody pulled his pistol and shot at the shooter but missed as well. The shooter bolted off away from him in the direction of Aiyana. The wolfpack was in close pursuit, but the rider was in a full gallop and started to distance himself from the pack. Cody fearing that he might reach Aiyana before he could catch him, hollered out to Blackred, "Let's go, boy, come on," and Blackred sprinted after the shooter with fire and rage.

It didn't take long before Cody caught up with the shooter. He lunged from Blackred, knocking the shooter off his horse. The two plummeted to the ground, tossed, and rolled hard until they stopped. Cody looked at the man and recognized him. "I know you," he said. "We fought together at the Battle of Shiloh." The Angel of Death looked at Cody and said, "You don't know me," then charged Cody, knocking him to the ground. He pulled his butcher knife and dove on top of Cody, but Cody was too strong and flipped him over onto his back and began punching the bounty man in the face. He kicked Cody back, got up, and charged toward Cody, but Cody used his momentum to flip him, slamming him into the ground. Cody got up, walked to Blackred, and pulled his bayonet from his saddle. When he turned, the bounty man was about to throw a knife at him, but the white wolf leaped from the rocks behind him, knocking over the bounty man and ripping the blade from his hand. The Angel of Death reached for the derringer in his right boot and pulled it out, aiming it at the white wolf. But before he could pull the trigger, Cody grabbed the gun and rammed his bayonet through the bounty man's throat in a swift blow. The blade pierced the skull of the Angel of Death. Then he pulled the bayonet out and watched as the bounty man's blood soiled the ground. Cody got up, looked over the dead man, and said, "This is what you get for shooting my wife."

The Angel of Death was dead! Death hovered over the dead man, opened a hole in Earth, and took his soul to the gateway of hell!

CHAPTER TWELVE

Bittersweet

God looks down from the heavens with tears of abatement. Human-kind's senseless self-destruction and evil greed reap havoc and endless waste. The world is marred by invisible boundaries manipulated by the dominant. Life can feel like the weight of the mountains is crushing your soul. Every day is another chance to survive; what doesn't kill you strengthens you! Cody looked over the dead bounty man and thought to himself, I knew him from the war. We fought the same battles. In war, you lose sight of who you are!

He said to himself as he mounted Blackred, "I hope you rot in hell, you bastard," and road off to find Aiyana. He turned, looked back at the dead bounty man, and watched the vultures eagerly feast on the fresh carcass.

Aiyana was resting near a tree close to a small fire. The spirit wolf and her pack were lying around her, watching intently as Cody and Blackred rode into camp. As he stepped off Blackred, the white wolf walked up to him. Cody knelt to pet her, and she reciprocated by licking his face. The gunslinger looked at her and said, "We are a good team, you and I," while scratching behind her ears. He looked up at Aiyana to see her smiling at him. He walked over to her, knelt to look at her wound, and said, "Let me see how this looks," but Aiyana pulled him to her lips, and the two kissed and hugged each other tightly. She prayed to the spirit gods, thanking them for their protection. Cody held her tight, kissed her forehead, and then tended her wounds.

Cody wasn't an expert in stitches but had learned a thing or two as a soldier. He made an excellent suture and then put an herb mixture on her wound to patch her up. He wrapped her with a fresh linen cloth as she admired him. She was in love for the first time in her life. When evening came, she held him close while they peered at the stars. They lay together near the fire and watched the shooting stars fall above the moonlit sky; it was a sign from the heavens! Cody plunged into a deep sleep and re-lived the moments during the war when he fought next to the bounty man. It was so vivid; he could reach out and touch him. Cody had never put two and two together before, but it started to make sense. All the stories of the bounty man and his killing spree meddled with his conscious. He had heard talk about a sinister man called the Angel of Death.

Opening his eyes, he looked at Aiyana asleep in his arms and thought to himself, *A second chance at love is more than destiny*. Cody and Aiyana stayed in their camp for two weeks while she recovered from her wound. Cody used his time hunting, fishing, and caring for Aiyana while she healed. He had found a nice piece of wood and whittled during the afternoons peacefully. One afternoon after cooking Aiyana some fresh venison, they enjoyed their meal together, then Cody pulled a cloth-wrapped bundle from his shirt, handed it to Aiyana with a smile, and said, "For you!" Her smile touched both ears as she sat up enthusiastically, unwrapping the cloth bundle. When she finally opened it, she looked in disbelief. The wooden box was beautiful, with little details carved on the sides and lid. There was an inscription carved on the top that read "Eternal Blossom." She opened the box lid, and the little music machine began to play a sparkling melody. She looked up at Cody with a tear in her eye and kissed him tenderly, and said, "*Aishen* (thank you)." Then she placed his hand on her belly and said, "*Bah bah*," she repeated the word, "*Bah bah*," and pressed Cody's hand tight against her stomach. Cody looked at Aiyana and picked her up, excitedly spinning her around, shouting, "We are going to have a baby." A tear rolled down his cheek in happiness!

The ride through the Garden of the Gods was breathtaking. They both marveled at the spectacular landscape as they headed south to Colorado Springs. When they arrived, they left the horses at the local stable and requested a new shod and bed in freshly cleaned stables. He escorted Aiyana to the "Antler's Hotel." The sign-out front read, "Best Hotel in These Parts." Cody booked a room for two days. Aiyana had never slept in a bed; she had never seen such a place adorned with beautiful furniture and antiquities. When they arrived at their room, the hotel servant opened the doors, and Aiyana entered speechless. The look on her face said it all. She walked around, touching the wood and curtains. Cody looked at the hotel servant and said, "Bring dinner for two, and fix a hot bath for my wife." Not long after, the hotel servant returned with dinner. Fresh quail was served with roasted potatoes and gravy sauce. They ate while the hotel servant filled the tub with fresh warm water, then she left a bar of lavender soap next to the tub. The servant went, and Cody helped remove Aiyana's soiled clothes and then helped her step into the tub.

Aiyana sunk into the water and succumbed to the incredible sensation of a warm bath. Cody grabbed the lavender soap bar and washed Aiyana's body gently, knowing she was with their child. He took the soap bar, lathered her hair, then slowly rinsed the soap revealing her beauty, and kissed her softly. He let her soak by herself for a while before joining her. The two relaxed in the hot tub and enjoyed the peace and tranquility of the moment together as a young family. The long ride to Texas would take nearly two months. Along the way, they stopped in Sweetwater for supplies. Cody bought a covered wagon with a horse from the local stables. He set up a bed for Aiyana to rest when they traveled the long flat lands of Texas.

They arrived at the Frio River and made camp for two days. They bathed in the cool spring water. The cold water was refreshing and a welcome break from the wretched heat. Cody noticed a slight belly bulge on Aiyana's stomach and knew he had to get to their destination soon. They found a small, secluded piece of land to homestead along the Frio River and built a small ranch. They had three kids, two boys and a little girl they named June. Cody called her little June bug. Blackred, the white wolf and her pack lived on the ranch watching over the small family and continued to protect them. There were moments when Cody reflected on Cheryl Lynn. He pulled out the small linen cloth she gave him that he kept in his pocket. It was a beautiful clear day. Cody looked out across the hills and noticed the eagle overhead. It was the first time he thought the past might have been left behind. He thought to himself, *trouble I'm sure to find*, and then he realized, *the devil didn't get the best of me!* He pressed the small cloth to his lips, smiled, and kissed a dream for two. A tear fell from his eye as he spoke to Cheryl Lynn in a low voice, "Life is bittersweet!"

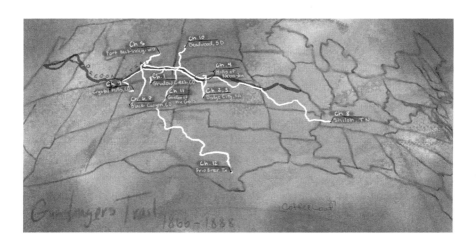